PRO HOCKEY'S

ALL-TIME GREATEST COMEBACKS

BY SEAN McCOLLUM

CONSULTANT:
BRUCE BERGLUND
PROFESSOR OF HISTORY, CALVIN COLLEGE
GRAND RAPIDS, MICHIGAN

CAPSTONE PRESS
a capstone imprint

Edge Books are published by Capstone Press
1710 Roe Crest Drive, North Mankato, Minnesota 56003
www.mycapstone.com

LIBRARY OF CONGRESS CATALOGING-IN-PUBLICATION DATA

Title: Pro hockey's all-time greatest comebacks / by Sean McCollum.
Description: Mankato, Minnesota : Capstone Press, [2019] | Series: Edge books. Sports comebacks | Includes bibliographical references and index.
Identifiers: LCCN 2018031868 (print) | LCCN 2018039935 (ebook) | ISBN 9781543554403 (eBook PDF) | ISBN 9781543554359 (library binding)
Subjects: LCSH: National Hockey League—History—Juvenile literature. | Hockey—History—Juvenile literature. | Comebacks—Juvenile literature.
Classification: LCC GV847.8.N3 (ebook) | LCC GV847.8.N3 M28 2019 (print) | DDC 796.962/64—dc23
LC record available at https://lccn.loc.gov/2018031868

Summary: Engaging text and action-packed photos describe the greatest comeback stories in National Hockey League history.

EDITORIAL CREDITS

Aaron Sautter, editor; Bob Lentz and Jennifer Bergstrom, designers; Eric Gohl, media researcher; Tori Abraham, production specialist

PHOTO CREDITS

Associated Press: 14, 18, Gene J. Puskar, 27, Matt Slocum, cover; Getty Images: Andrew D. Bernstein, 22, Brian Babineau, 6, Bruce Bennett, 9, Noah Graham, 11, Steve Babineau, 5; Newscom: Cal Sport Media/Scott D Stivason, 20, MCT/Chuck Myers, 28–29, Reuters/Brian Snyder, 17, Reuters/Gary Hershorn, 24, ZUMA Press/Bildbyran, 12; Shutterstock: Shooter Bob Square Lenses, 1

Design Elements: Shutterstock

Printed and bound in the United States of America.
PA48

TABLE OF CONTENTS

THE LAST LAUGH

One goal . . . two goals . . . three . . . UGH! Watching your favorite National Hockey League (NHL) team fall behind is agony. You wish you could do something, anything, to help your hockey heroes get back in the game.

Boston Bruins fans had that gloomy, sinking feeling in Round 1 of the 2013 Stanley Cup playoffs. Their team trailed the Toronto Maple Leafs 4–1 in the third period of Game 7.

However, the Bruins weren't ready to quit. On the next **shift**, Boston found the net to make the score 4–2. Suddenly a buzz of hope ran through the crowd. Now the Bruins just had to finish the job.

An old saying claims that, "The one who laughs last, laughs best." For hockey fans on the right side of a comeback, there's nothing better than being the last one laughing.

---

shift—the period of time a player or line is on the ice before being replaced by another

The Boston Bruins fiercely attacked the Toronto Maple Leafs' net to keep their hopes alive in the 2013 Stanley Cup playoffs.

CHAPTER 1

GREAT RINK RALLIES

Seeing your favorite team get a solid win is satisfying. Winning a squeaker can be tense, yet exciting. But for hockey fans, nothing is more thrilling than seeing your team come from behind to snatch victory from the jaws of defeat.

THE BOSTON OT PARTY

Down 4–2 to Toronto in Game 7, it was do or die time for the Bruins and their 2013 playoff hopes. With time running out, Boston emptied its net, pulling goalie Tuukka Rask to get an extra attacker on the ice.

With 1:22 left, the desperation move paid off. Milan Lucic got his stick on a rebound and scored. The Maple Leafs' lead was down to one. Half a minute later, the Bruins were again on the attack. Patrice Bergeron fired a laser shot into the net, tying the game and sending it into sudden-death **overtime**. The first team to score would win.

The Bruins had all the momentum as the puck dropped on the extra period. Like furious black-and-yellow bees, they trapped the Maple Leafs on their half of the ice. At 6:05 in OT, a loose puck deflected to Bergeron and he slapped it home. The home crowd erupted as Boston completed an amazing comeback.

Boston had won Game 7 after being down by three goals in the third period. It was the first time any team had ever accomplished that feat. The Bruins went on to play in the Stanley Cup Finals. But their luck ran out there, losing to the Chicago Blackhawks.

---

overtime—an extra period of play if the score is tied at the end of three periods

CANADIEN COMEBACK

The legendary Montreal Canadiens team was first formed in 1909. The team has a long history, but one 1971 playoff game against the Bruins saw the Canadiens' greatest highlight.

The Canadiens faced the defending champion Bruins in the first round of the Stanley Cup playoffs. It didn't look good for Montreal early in the series. Led by superstars Phil Esposito and Bobby Orr, Boston's powerful lineup had set scoring records during the regular season. The Bruins took Game 1, and in Game 2 they jumped to a 5–1 lead. Boston seemed to be unstoppable. But with about 4:30 left in the second period, Montreal center Henri Richard stole the puck. He raced in for the score to make it 5–2.

In the third period, the Canadiens found their groove. Montreal scored five straight goals against the regular season's best team. Final score: 7–5. It is considered the greatest comeback in the Canadiens' long history. They then went on to win the series.

Montreal didn't rest on that upset, though. They knocked off the Minnesota North Stars in the second round. Then they bested the Chicago Blackhawks to hoist the Stanley Cup.

A TRUE DYNASTY

The Canadiens have won the Stanley Cup 24 times, more than any other team.

Center Jean Béliveau scored two of the Canadiens' seven goals during their big comeback win.

SHARK ATTACK

In Round 1 of the 2011 Stanley Cup playoffs, the Los Angeles Kings seemed to be in control of their own destiny. It was Game 3 of the series against the San Jose Sharks. Early in the second period, Brad Richardson scored to increase the Kings' lead to 4–0.

But the rest of that period became one of the wildest in NHL history. The Sharks finally seemed to find their teeth. They scored three straight to come within a goal of the Kings. Los Angeles bounced right back to add a goal of its own. But then the Sharks counter-attacked and racked up two more. At the end of two periods, the score was knotted up 5–5. In the third period, neither team would bend, and the game went to overtime.

Just three minutes into the extra period, the Sharks' Patrick Marleau made a sweet cross-ice pass to teammate Devin Setoguchi. The Kings' goalie laid out on the ice to block it. But the shot was already in the net.

The Sharks' furious comeback was complete. They were only the third team in Stanley Cup history to come back from four goals down to win a game.

Devin Setoguchi fired the puck past Kings goalie Jonathan Quick to give the Sharks a 6–5 overtime win.

MIRACLE ON MANCHESTER

In a 1982 playoff game, the Kings won after trailing the Edmonton Oilers by five goals. It is remembered as "The Miracle on Manchester" because the Kings' arena was on Manchester Boulevard. It is still the biggest single-game comeback in NHL playoff history.

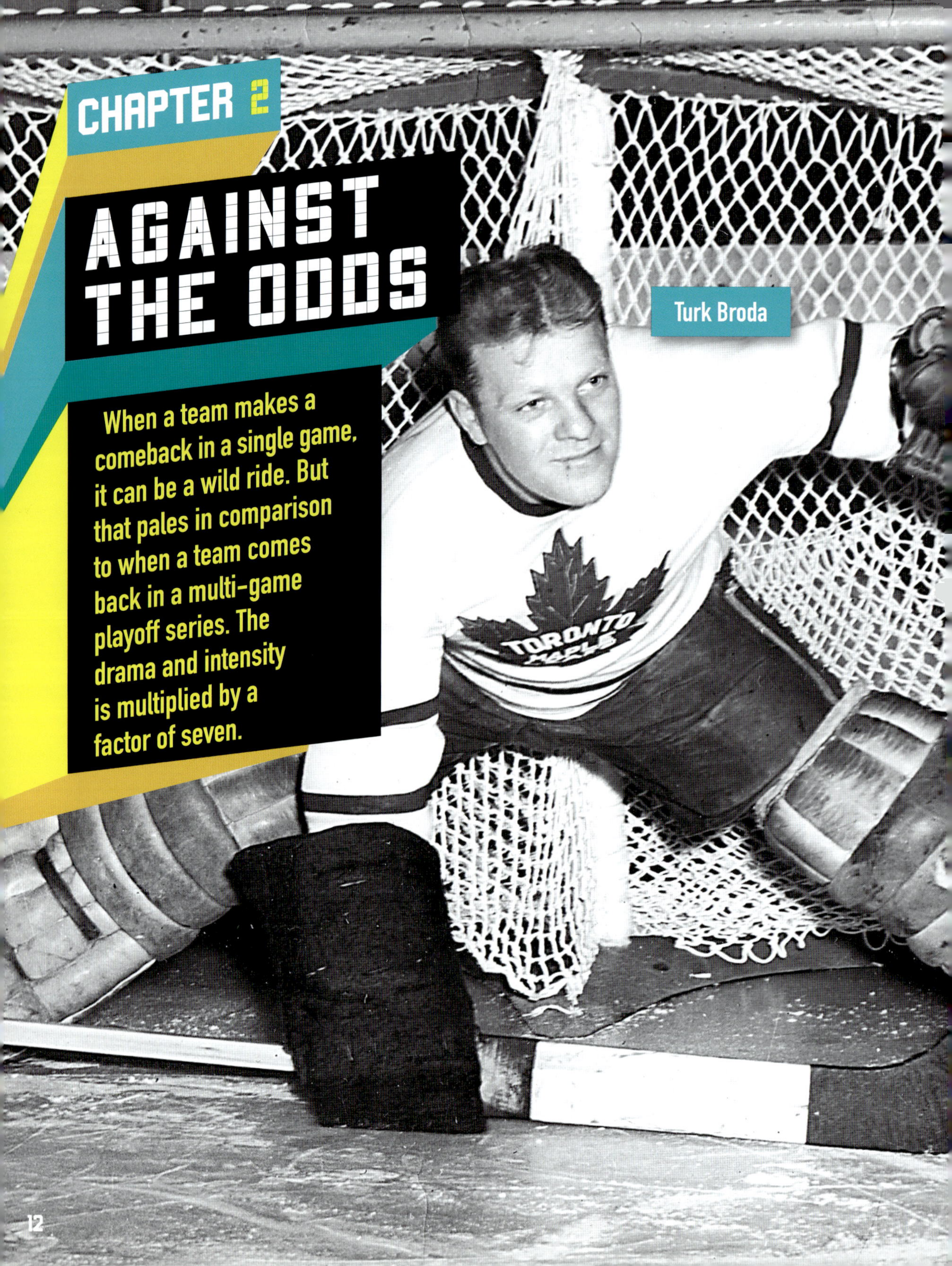

CHAPTER 2

AGAINST THE ODDS

When a team makes a comeback in a single game, it can be a wild ride. But that pales in comparison to when a team comes back in a multi-game playoff series. The drama and intensity is multiplied by a factor of seven.

Turk Broda

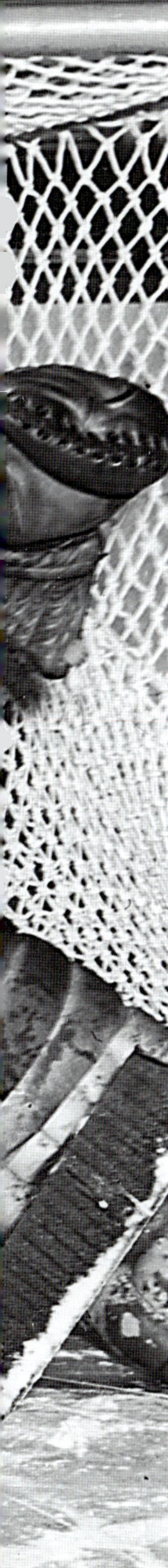

MAPLE LEAF MIRACLE

The Detroit Red Wings were well on their way to winning the 1942 Stanley Cup. They had already taken a 3 to 0 series lead over the Toronto Maple Leafs.

Detroit continued to dominate in Game 4. The Red Wings led 3–2 in the third period. Detroit fans readied their brooms to celebrate the team's **sweep**. But then Toronto scored two goals to stay alive with a 4–3 win. And they didn't stop there. Somehow, the momentum had swung Toronto's way. The Maple Leafs walloped Detroit 9–5 in Game 5. Then behind the great play of goalie Turk Broda, they blanked the Red Wings 3–0 in Game 6.

The all-or-nothing Game 7 started out as a defensive battle. The two teams dueled to a 0–0 tie in the first period. Detroit got on the board first with a goal late in the second period. But Toronto's Sweeney Schriner put one in the net to tie it early in the third. Then Pete Langelle and Schriner added two more goals to complete the Leafs' epic comeback and win the Cup. The Maple Leafs had won four in a row after being down three games. No NHL club has yet repeated that feat in the Stanley Cup Finals.

---

sweep—when a team wins all the games in a series without losing to the opposing team

Rookie goalie Glenn Resch was like a brick wall in the 1975 playoffs. Against the Pittsburgh Penguins he allowed just four goals and blocked 124 shots.

Glenn Resch

THE ISLANDERS GROW UP

Bing. Bang. Boom. Just like that, the New York Islanders were down three games to none against the Pittsburgh Penguins. Things looked bleak for the Islanders in the second round of the 1975 playoffs. But the Islanders weren't going to go away quietly.

In Game 4, the Islanders' coach switched goalies to Glenn "Chico" Resch. The rookie played great, allowing just four goals in Games 4, 5, and 6. The Islanders won all of them.

Game 7 was back in Pittsburgh. Again, Resch's play behind the pads was inspired. Several near misses by the Penguins dinged off the goalposts. Resch was so relieved he kissed the pipes. In the end, he shut out Pittsburgh in a 1–0 game that **clinched** the series.

New York became just the second NHL team to charge back and win after being down three games in the playoffs. The Islanders fell to the Philadelphia Flyers in the next round. But they were growing toward greatness. From 1980–1983 they claimed four straight Stanley Cup titles.

clinch—to secure a victory in a competition

FLYING HIGH

The Boston Bruins had the Philadelphia Flyers right where they wanted them. The Bruins were up three games to zip in the 2010 Eastern Conference Semifinals.

The Flyers weren't ready to cash in their season just yet, though. They pulled out a 5–4 nail-biter to win Game 4 in overtime. In Game 5 the Flyers' goalies teamed up to beat the Bruins in a 4–0 **shutout**. Then a 2–1 victory in Game 6 set up a do-or-die Game 7.

In the final game, Boston built a 3–0 lead in the first period on a pair of **power-play** goals. The Flyers managed to notch one score before the end of the period. They added a pair of goals in the second period to catch up to Boston. In the third period, the Bruins got called for a crucial penalty. The Flyers scored a goal on the following power play, which proved to be the game-winner. The Flyers became the third NHL team ever to overcome a three-game **deficit** in the Stanley Cup playoffs.

---

shutout—when a team doesn't score

power play—when a team has a one- or two-player advantage because the other team has players in the penalty box

deficit—an amount of points that a team is behind by in a game

Simon Gagne

Flyers left wing Simon Gagne made the game-winning goal against the Bruins with just over seven minutes remaining in the game.

COMEBACK KINGS

In 2014 the L.A. Kings became the fourth team to come back from 0–3 to win a seven-game playoff series. They shocked the San Jose Sharks in the first round.

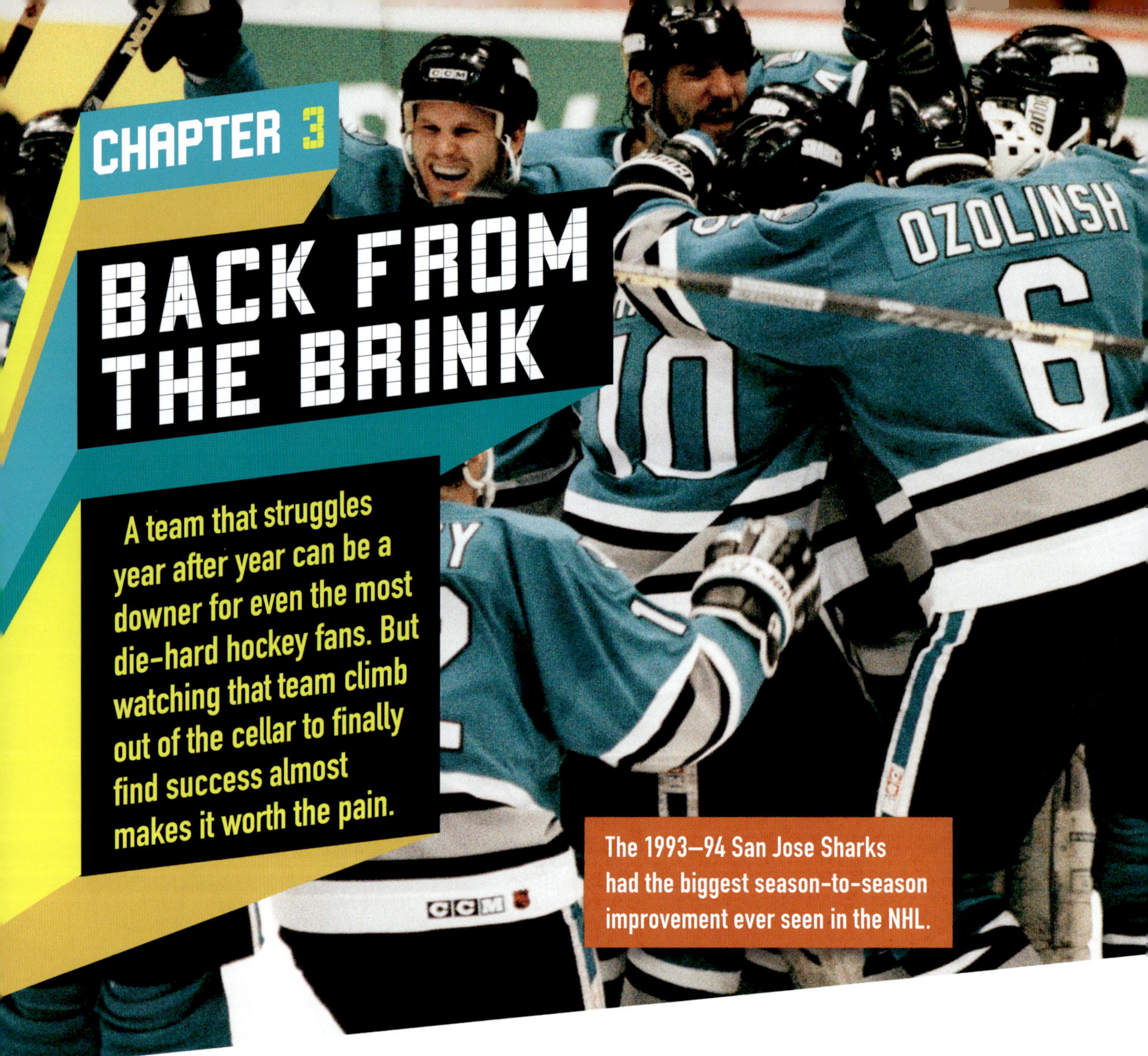

CHAPTER 3
BACK FROM THE BRINK

A team that struggles year after year can be a downer for even the most die-hard hockey fans. But watching that team climb out of the cellar to finally find success almost makes it worth the pain.

The 1993–94 San Jose Sharks had the biggest season-to-season improvement ever seen in the NHL.

UP FROM THE DEEP

In the 1992–93 season, the San Jose Sharks were bottom feeders. They won only 11 games and lost 71 that year, a league record, and had two ties. The team totaled just 24 points in the standings (2 points for a win, 1 point for a tie).

But what a difference a year can make. Entering the 1993–94 season, the Sharks had a new coach. They also got a new arena, nicknamed the Shark Tank. The coach rebuilt the **roster** to give the team a more balanced attack. The Sharks tripled their wins to 33 and totaled 82 points for the season. The 58-point surge from the year before was a record rise for an NHL franchise.

But even more impressive is what came next. The Sharks managed to squeeze into the playoffs as the last seed. In Round 1 they faced off against the powerful Detroit Red Wings. In one of the biggest upsets in NHL history, San Jose beat the Wings in seven games. In Round 2 the Sharks pushed the Toronto Maple Leafs to seven games, but came up one win short of moving on to the next playoff round.

DOUBLE POINTS

Only one other team has improved by more than 50 points between seasons. The Quebec Nordiques doubled their total from 52 points in 1991–92 to 104 in 1992–93.

roster—a list of players on a team

Colorado Avalanche center Nathan MacKinnon faces off against Nashville Predators left wing Viktor Arvidsson in the 2018 Stanley Cup playoffs.

COLORADO CLIMBING

Over the years the Colorado Avalanche have had a lot of success. They've often appeared in the NHL playoffs and have won two Stanley Cup titles. But the 2016–17 season was a big disappointment. The team finished last in its division with just 22 wins and scored the fewest points in its history with 48.

There was nowhere for the Avs to go but up. They hired a new coach and added speedy young players to the roster. In the 2017–18 season the team sent 11 different rookies onto the ice. The changes had a positive impact. The Avs went 43–30 on the season and totaled 95 points. Their 47-point jump was the fourth largest in NHL history.

The Avalanche capped their comeback season by making the playoffs as a **wild card** team. They lost to the Nashville Predators in the first round. However, like all rebuilding teams, they had taken a huge step toward creating a winning future.

wild card—a team that has not won its division but qualifies for an open spot in the playoffs

A WINNING MOVE

In 1995 the Quebec Nordiques moved to Denver, Colorado, to become the Avalanche. They won the Stanley Cup in their first season in their new city.

Wayne Gretzky

CHAPTER 4

HOCKEY HEROES RETURN

It takes a total team effort to come back for a big win. Unfortunately, players sometimes face struggles that keep them from helping their team. However, the courage of one player making a personal comeback can sometimes lift up the entire team.

THE GREAT ONE RETURNS

Most hockey fans feel that Wayne Gretzky was the best player in history. Including the playoffs, he set records for goals (1,016), assists (2,223), and points (3,239) that lead all other players by a wide margin.

However, just before the start of the 1992–93 season "the Great One" faced a challenge he couldn't outskate. He injured his back and was in terrible pain. Even sitting was unbearable.

Still, Gretzky fought through it. He was back on the ice after missing 39 games. The Los Angeles Kings struggled, but squeaked into the playoffs.

The Kings and Gretzky then began playing their best hockey of the year. The Kings powered through the first two rounds of the playoffs. They downed both the Calgary Flames and Vancouver Canucks in six games.

The Kings next faced the Toronto Maple Leafs in the Western Conference Finals. In Game 6 Gretzky scored the winning goal in overtime. He then hung up a **hat trick** in Game 7, leading his team to a 5–4 victory and a trip to the Stanley Cup Finals. But the Kings' luck had run out. The Montreal Canadiens beat the Kings in five games. Still, Gretzky's magical return to the ice had inspired the Kings to make a serious run at the title.

THE GREAT ONE

Wayne Gretzky retired in 1999. He was inducted into the NHL Hall of Fame that same year. He currently holds a whopping 60 NHL records.

hat trick—when a player scores three goals in one game

Steve Yzerman

THE CAPTAIN COMES BACK

Steve Yzerman had paid his dues. He joined the Detroit Red Wings in 1983 at age 18. And he became team captain at just 21. Yzerman was a great scorer who developed into one of the best defensive forwards in the NHL. The Red Wings had gone 42 years without winning the Stanley Cup. That **drought** ended in 1997 with Yzerman leading the way.

But by the 2001–02 season his body was feeling 18 years of wear and tear. A bad right knee was slowing him down, and he missed 30 regular season games.

Yzerman could hardly walk, but he was back on skates when the playoffs started. In the opening round, the Wings dropped the first two games to the Vancouver Canucks. Yzerman **rallied** his team, and they came back to tie and then win the series. The Red Wings next knocked off the St. Louis Blues and the Avalanche to reach the Stanley Cup Finals. Detroit then sealed the deal by beating the Carolina Hurricanes. Yzerman's teammates credited his physical courage and leadership for inspiring their championship run.

---

drought—a long period in which a team does not win a title

rally—to come from behind to tie or take the lead in a game

SUPER MARIO

Mario Lemieux was one of the best hockey players ever to lace up skates. He was a wizard with the stick. He led the Pittsburgh Penguins to Stanley Cup titles in 1991 and 1992. When he retired he held 14 Penguins team records.

His hockey career is even more remarkable considering his setbacks. During the 1992–93 season, Lemieux learned he had Hodgkin's lymphoma, a type of blood cancer. He missed two months of the season for treatment. He returned in time to lead the Penguins to the playoffs.

In 1993 Lemieux had back surgery and missed most of the season and the entire following season. Many fans wondered if Lemieux's stellar career was over. But he made another comeback in 1995–96 and tallied 161 points. He was the league's top scorer that year.

Mario Lemieux **retired** after the 1997 season. Then in 1999 he bought the Penguins to keep the team in Pittsburgh. Lemieux made a third comeback when he came out of retirement in 2000 and led his team to the 2001 Eastern Conference Finals. He finally hung up his skates for good in 2006 to focus on running the team as an owner.

retire—to give up a line of work

WINNING OWNER

Under Lemieux's ownership the Penguins won Stanley Cup titles in 2009, 2016, and 2017. He is the only person to have his name on the Cup as both a player and a team owner.

EXTRA SHOTS:

MORE INCREDIBLE COMEBACKS

MR. HOCKEY: Gordie Howe was often known as "Mr. Hockey." Howe was a beloved NHL star. He played his first game in 1946 and retired—the first time—in 1971. But he came back two years later to play with his two sons for the Houston Aeros in the World Hockey Association. He later returned to the NHL with the Hartford Whalers for one last season in 1979–80. He finally retired for good at the age of 52. He is the only NHL player to have played in five different decades.

U.S. WOMEN'S HOCKEY, 1998: The 1998 Olympics was the first to include women's hockey. Team USA and Team Canada faced off in the first round. Canada took control of the game, carrying a 4–1 lead into the third period. Then the American women turned the tables. They scored six goals in 12 minutes and won 7–4. The two squads played a rematch three days later, this time for the gold medal. Final score: USA 3, Canada 1.

NCAA HOCKEY CHAMPIONSHIP, 2009: With 3:30 left in the third period, the Boston University Terriers pulled their goalie off the ice. They trailed Miami (Ohio) University 3–1 in the NCAA Championship game and needed a miracle. BU's Zach Cohen gave them a glimmer of hope when he scored with less than a minute to go. Then with just 17 seconds on the clock, Nick Bonino tied it to force overtime. In OT a shot deflected off a Miami player and found the net to complete the miracle comeback.

Marie-Philip Poulin

CANADIAN WOMEN'S HOCKEY, 2014: At the 2014 Olympics, Team USA and Team Canada faced off once again. This time it was in the gold medal game. Team USA scored early in the third period for a 2–0 lead. Team Canada scored to draw within one. Then with just 90 seconds left Canada replaced their goalie with an extra attacker. Marie-Philip Poulin scored the tying goal to send the game into overtime. In OT, she converted on a power play to make the game-winning shot.

GLOSSARY

clinch (KLINCH)—to secure a victory in a competition

deficit (DEF-uh-sit)—an amount of points that a team is behind by in a game

drought (DROUT)—a long period in which a team does not win a title

hat trick (HAT TRIK)—when a player scores three goals in one game

overtime (OH-vur-time)—an extra period of play if the score is tied at the end of three periods

power play (POW-ur PLAY)—when a team has a one- or two-player advantage because the other team has players in the penalty box

rally (RAL-ee)—to come from behind to tie or take the lead in a game

retire (ri-TIRE)—to give up a line of work

roster (ROSS-tur)—a list of players on a team

shift (SHIFT)—the period of time a player or line is on the ice before being replaced by another

shutout (SHUHT-out)—when a team doesn't score

sweep (SWEEP)—when a team wins all the games in a series without losing to the opposing team

wild card (WILD kahrd)—a team that has not won its division but qualifies for an open spot in the playoffs

READ MORE

Bradley, Michael. *Pro Hockey's Underdogs: Players and Teams Who Shocked the Hockey World.* Sports Shockers! North Mankato, Minn.: Capstone Press, 2018.

Hoena, Blake. *Lake Placid Miracle: When U.S. Hockey Stunned the World.* Greatest Sports Moments. North Mankato, Minn.: Capstone Press, 2018.

Page, Sam. *Hockey: Then to Wow!* New York: Liberty Street, an imprint of Time Inc. Books, 2017.

INTERNET SITES

Use FactHound to find Internet sites related to this book.

1. Visit *www.facthound.com*

2. Just type in 9781543554359 and go.

INDEX